About the Author

Nicky Nicholls would love to be an F1 Driver or an Intergalactic Explorer but is currently enjoying working as an Intervention and Drama Teacher at a primary school in London. She lives in South East London, with her family and Dave the Cat.

About the Illustrator

Georgina is an Artist and Illustrator, who lives in Saddleworth with family and pets and recommends putting your socks on the radiator at night, so they'll be warm in the morning when you put them on.

The Boy Who Sneezed To Space

Written by Nicky Nicholls
Illustrated by Georgina 'Ed' Lambert
Typesetting by Jeremy Nicholls

_____

The Boy Who Sneezed To Space

www.olympiapublishers.com
OLYMPIA PAPERBACK EDITION

Copyright © Nicky Nicholls 2020
Illustrations by Georgina Ed Lambert

A CIP catalogue record for this title is available from the British Library.

ISBN: 978-1-78830-593-8
First Published in 2020

Olympia Publishers
Tallis House
2 Tallis Street
London
EC4Y 0AB

Printed in Great Britain

Dedication

For Jez – NN
For Mary and Graham & Dora and George – GL

James was sitting down to breakfast, on a morning before school, when something odd took hold of him whilst sat there on his stool.

It started at the bottom and then wriggled to the top, he wondered if the feeling would ever, ever stop.

Then she looked up at the ceiling
and it all became quite clear.
Young James was hurtling up and up
and heading out to space,
the last he saw of Mum
was the confused look on her face!

He blasted through the atmosphere 'til the Earth was just a ball.
It was blue and green and beautiful but was getting rather small.

Beyond the Earth, towards the sun he saw Mercury and Venus, the closest planets to the Sun he looked at them with keenness.

Mercury the closest, was the smallest one by far, James could see it clearly now and it felt so bizarre!

He noticed that it had no moons and a surface full of craters, it looked like it had been attacked by a million alligators.

Up next, its neighbour Venus, known as the sister planet of Earth,
as although it spins the other way, they're of similar mass and girth.
James knew that in the Solar System, this was the hottest planet,
along with its great poisonous clouds, it was impossible to inhabit.

James continued his journey to the stars, heading away from the Sun,
he couldn't wait to tell his friends, he was having so much fun!

The red planet Mars was now in his sights, it looked incredibly rusty.
Named after the Roman God of War this planet was rocky and dusty.

With its two moons and old streambeds, could aliens really live there? James imagined

The gas giant Jupiter now loomed into view, with its giant red spot raging.
A gigantic storm, that's been fuming for years and shows no signs of aging.

Orbiting round it were many moons,
including the Galilean four;

Ganymede

Europa

Callisto

"Woo Hoo!" said James as the rings of Saturn now came into sight.
He remembered Saturn was made of gases that make it incredibly light.

The rings around - made of ice and rock - were spectacular and grand,
they varied in size from the size of a house, to the size of a grain of sand.

As well as planets James enjoyed seeing the beautiful bright stars.
Asteroids went whizzing past like flying, speeding cars.

Just then, unlike the other

planets, spinning on its side, was Uranus!

"Look it's blue and ringed! I love it! WOW!" James cried.

It reminded him of his marbles at home it looked so smooth and perfect,

but he knew that it was incredibly cold and winds blew all around it.

The furthest planet from the Sun was now coming into view,
Neptune was casting all around a beautiful blue hue.

James knew that this ice giant, took the longest to orbit the sun

He knew of the planet's violent storms that were crazy, windy and wild.

During this time James was travelling at an enormous speed.
The trouble was he was starting to feel such a burning need,
to get home and see his friends, his sister, dad and mum.
"How will I get home now?" he thought, feeling rather sad and glum.

"I've seen Mercury, Venus, Earth and Mars, comets, moons, asteroids and stars,

Just at this point an odd creature flew by.
An alien with tentacles, spots and one eye.

When it moved it wobbled like a plate load of jelly,
glowing bright pink and green with an oval shaped belly.

It was in a golden spaceship, flying faster than light, but on seeing James, who made such a
sorrowful sight, stopped its craft next to him and spoke alienese. James smiled, tried explaining

He gestured his tentacles towards his gold rocket, and fished out the keys from his jelly lined pocket.
He waved them at James to show his intention, towards the spacecraft (his own great invention).

James understood what the alien meant
and crawled in to wait for the speedy descent.

On a space map James showed Goon his hometown,
he was so excited, he was going to get down.

He watched Goon press buttons and pull levers galore,
then the force of the launch pushed him onto the floor.

From the porthole he saw the planets shoot past,
they were going like the clappers, unbelievably fast!
They zoomed fast past comets, asteroids and stars,
now they were flying past the red planet Mars
and there James saw Earth, a comforting ball,
with his house, friends and family, how he'd missed them all.

His family sat down to tea, his favourite chips and beans.
Hungrily he shoved food in like a bean munching machine.
But suddenly his tummy lurched and it made him feel quite weird.

And just like that James shot straight back up, with a resounding

FART!

Disclaimer from the author.

Dear Reader,

I have had immense pleasure writing this book and whilst most the information is correct, remember they are discovering new things about space all the time. Also, it should be said that my imagination has taken artistic licence at times: please take note of the following!

- James wouldn't be able to see the Earth as 'just a ball' when he blasts through the atmosphere. The atmosphere ends just 100km up, so in order to see the Earth as 'just a ball' you'd need to be much further away.
- Although, in the story, James laughs and talks in space, sadly this is not possible. This is because there is no air in space so consequently the sound has no way of travelling. So never mind laughing and talking, James wouldn't actually be able to breathe!
- Although James says he can 'see Earth's moon from Saturn,' he wouldn't be able to, as it would be invisible from this far away.
- You never know, Goon and his fellow aliens may well have found a way to supply the infinite amount of energy needed to fly his self-made rocket 'faster than light'. However, on Earth we have not, so doing so is an impossibility. Shame I know!
- As for aliens and giants in space... who knows? I like to think they exist but as yet there is no evidence to suggest that they do... or that they don't!

It goes without saying - don't try this at home! Sneezing or farting into space is not to be recommended.

Best of Wishes

    Nicky